FEB - - 2017   W9-CKW-505

Parents and Caregivers,

Stone Arch Readers are designed to provide enjoyable reading experiences, as well as opportunities to develop vocabulary, literacy skills, and comprehension. Here are a few ways to support your beginning reader:

• Talk with your child about the ideas addressed in the story.

• Discuss each illustration, mentioning the characters, where they are, and what they are doing.

• Read with expression, pointing to each word. You may want to read the whole story through and then revisit parts of the story to ensure that the meanings of words or phrases are understood.

• Talk about why the character did what he or she did and what your child would do in that situation.

• Help your child connect with characters and events in the story.

Remember, reading with your child should be fun, not forced. Each moment spent reading with your child is a priceless investment in his or her literacy life.

Gail Saunders-Smith, Ph.D.

Stone Arch Readers

are published by Stone Arch Books

a Capstone Imprint

1710 Roe Crest Drive

North Mankato, Minnesota 56003

www.capstonepub.com

Library of Congress Cataloging-in-Publication Data

Yasuda, Anita.

The slime attack / by Anita Yasuda ; illustrated by Steve Harpster.

p. cm. -- (Stone Arch readers: Dino detectives)

Summary: Ty loves to experiment, but when his friends arrive there is slime everywhere
and Ty has disappeared--so the Dino Detectives swing into action.

ISBN 978-1-4342-4153-5 (library binding) -- ISBN 978-1-4342-4833-6 (pbk.)

1. Dinosaurs--Juvenile fiction. 2. Science--Experiments--Juvenile fiction. [1. Dinosaurs--Fiction.
2. Experiments--Fiction. 3. Mystery and detective stories.] I. Harpster, Steve, ill.
II. Title.

PZ7.Y2124Sli 2013

813.6--dc23

2012027054

Reading Consultants:

Gail Saunders-Smith, Ph.D.

Melinda Melton Crow, M.Ed.

Laurie K. Holland, Media Specialist

Designer: Russell Griesmer

Printed in the United States of America in Stevens Point, Wisconsin.

092012

006937WZS13

The Slime Attack

by **Anita Yasuda**
illustrated by **Steve Harpster**

STONE ARCH BOOKS
a capstone imprint

Meet the Dino Detectives!

Dot the
Diplodocus

Sara the
Triceratops

Cory the
Corythosaurus

Ty the
T. rex

Ty loves to make things. He wants to make something special for his friends.

Ty runs to his lab. He has the perfect idea!

Ty puts on his lab coat. He puts on his glasses.

He pulls out his tools. Ty is ready to work.

Ty uses a pinch of this. Ty uses a dash of that.

"It needs one more thing,"
says Ty.

Plop! There is fizz. Plop! Plop!
There are bubbles. Then there are
more bubbles.

Then there is a loud boom!

Just then, Cory, Sara, and Dot knock on the door.

"What was that loud noise?"
asks Dot.

"I don't know," says Sara.

They walk into Ty's lab. Slime
is everywhere!

"Where's Ty?" asks Sara.

"Oh no!" says Dot. "Ty made a slime monster and it ate Ty!"

"The Dino Detectives can crack this case," says Cory. "Let's find some clues."

Sara finds Ty's lab coat. Dot
finds his glasses.

Cory finds some green tracks. The tracks go up the stairs. Then down the hall and into the bathroom.

"The tracks stop in the
bathroom," says Cory.

Then they hear a loud crash.

They tiptoe down the hall.
They stop at the closed door.

They knock on the door. They
hear a small moaning noise.

Cory slowly opens the door.

Ty is under a pile of books,
toys, and clothes.

"What happened?" asks Cory.

"I was trying to make slime cupcakes," he says. "They blew up. I had to take a shower to get clean."

"Why were you on the floor?"
asks Sara.

"I tripped and crashed," says Ty.

"We thought a slime monster ate you," says Dot.

"A slime monster? Now that's
a great idea for an invention,"
says Ty.

"One idea at a time," says
Cory.

Everyone laughs.

STORY WORDS

detectives   monster   invention

idea   tiptoe

Total Word Count: 293